Growing ♥ur hearts:

New Baby, New Groove

Written by Alishea Jurado and Frank Jurado (Mr. J)

Illustrated by Ellie Beykzadeh

Published by JamTree Publishing, LLC

Written by Alishea Jurado and Frank Jurado (Mr. J)

www.jamtreepublishing.com

jamtreepublishing@gmail.com

Follow Us: @dr.alisheajurado

Illustrations Copyright © 2023 by Ellie I. Beykzadeh

Illustrated by Ellie Beykzadeh

www.elliecolors.com

Follow Us: @elliecolorss

ISBN:
979-8-9889345-0-9 (Hardcover)
979-8-9889345-1-6 (Paperback)
979-8-9889345-2-3 (ebook)
Library of Congress Control Number 2023916423
First printing edition 2023
Printed in the U.S.A.

Miles and Quinn– Though your details and families differ, you each found yourself full of curiosity, wonder, and concern at the thought of welcoming a new baby. Miles– Cole is inspired by you everyday. He embodies your kindness, creativity, humor, and joy in all he does. Quinn– Keaton is forever laughing with and in awe of his older sister and magic maker. What a beautiful journey it has been watching you both find your groove as older siblings. Cole and Keaton– It is hard to imagine life without your melodies wrapped around us.
–Mama/PLP (Alishea)

In my life's symphony, you emerged as a captivating counterpoint, redefining the very essence of my melody. As my little conductor you continually lead my heart's orchestra to magnificent crescendos of growth, love and harmony. This book is for you, my maestro of joy, a timeless refrain of the incredible symphony we've composed together. I love you always, my "Sweet Baby James".
–Dada (Frank)

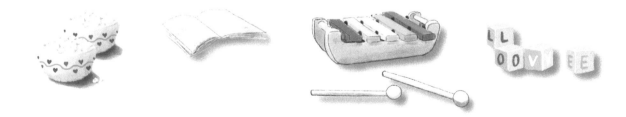

When people pass Mommy,
they give her a smile.
They open up doors.
They chat for a while.

They love her big belly,
and all want to know
what I think of the fact
that our family will grow.

It's a really good question;
I'm not sure, you see,
what it means for us all–
but especially for me.

When we go to the park,
will we still swing so high
and still lie on our backs
and count clouds in the sky?

Will we still dance together
and shimmy-shake move?
Or will new baby's beats
change the way that we groove?

Will she still tummy-tickle
till I loud-laughing snort,
with snacks set for two
in our pillow-couch fort?

Will we still splash in puddles
while rain drippy-drops,
arms fluttering free
while four feet hippy-hop?

Will she still read me stories
and sing to me, too?
Will new baby need Mommy
the way that I do?

Mommy says not to worry;
the most special part
about having new babies
is growing our hearts!

When we go to the park
we'll count clouds and swing high,
while sweet baby babbles
float their way toward the sky.

We'll still dance together
and shimmy-shake move
because new baby's beats
only spice up our groove!

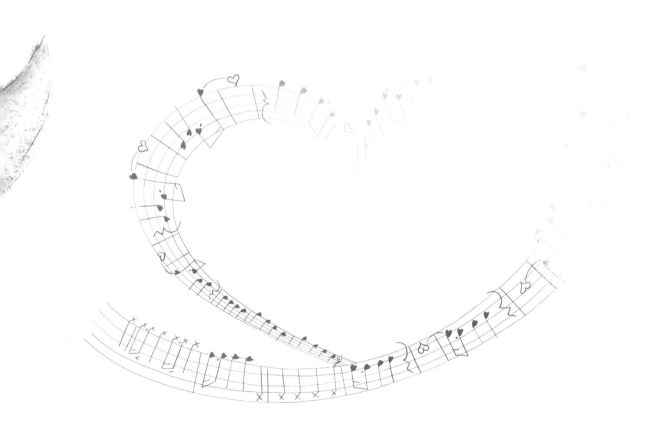

She'll still tummy-tickle
till I loud-laughing snort,
with snacks set for three
in our pillow-couch fort.

We'll still splash in puddles
as rain drippy-drops,
arms fluttering free
while six feet hippy-hop.

We'll still read together
and sing songs with new coos.
We'll both need our Mommy,
and she'll need us both, too!

She'll always love baby
and always love me,
and we'll grow enough love
for our whole family.

NOTE TO READER

Dear Reader,

Being a part of a family is a little like being in a band. We each bring our unique personalities, strengths, and roles, coming together to create a harmonious groove. Disagreements and challenges are part of the journey, but when we find our rhythm and harmony, we get to put on another epic show!

Similarly, adding a new sibling to the family is like adding a new member to the band. New ideas, talents, and insights add new layers and tempos to familiar tunes. This book addresses the raw and crucial questions that may arise when preparing to welcome another child into the family. How will our roles change? Will there be enough love for everyone? How will a new baby change our groove? In our experience, each new family member helps us grow and create dynamic textures and sounds we couldn't have imagined.

We've also realized that family life is full of improvisation- there is no sticking to a planned set list. We've learned to listen to each other, give space for solos, and trust and follow each other's lead. This takes so much practice and is why our fox sibling emerges in the illustrations a bit older than a baby. This timeline is different for every family, but there will be a point where you find your groove together, or, perhaps, the groove will find you!

In Love & Music,
Alishea and Frank

P.S. Let's keep grooving! Visit us at www.jamtreepublishing.com to access a sing-along and additional activities to extend and enrich this conversation.

FRANK JURADO

"Frank is undeniably one of the most remarkable individuals I know. His vibrant energy and infectious humor brighten every room as he effortlessly transforms any moment into an adventure. As a professionally trained musician and songwriter, he is extraordinarily talented. He brings this expertise and passion to children's music. Whether captivating a school audience, celebrating a birthday, or orchestrating a family jam class, he weaves a sense of community and collaboration through every event. His ability to personalize every musical experience to the hearts in front of him is truly a gift. You can find him in Miami playing ukulele while riding his one wheel by the ocean. It's a sibling dream to be able to collaborate with my amazing brother, a creative dynamo and rockstar, as we bring our stories to life through music." – Alishea, co-author and sister

ALISHEA JURADO

"Born in Puerto Rico and raised in Miami, my sister, Alishea, was destined to shine / The eldest of three in a magical family, the singer, director, and master of rhyme / As we grew and we learned how to share and take turns, she found new ways to bring us together / We felt safe, we felt love, with adventures and hugs, and a magical childhood I treasure / On her journey she flew as she learned and she grew, she would write the most beautiful songs / On the keys and the strings she would play and she'd sing, paving paths I would journey upon. I'm so thankful to be working with Alishea on our children's books and passion projects. Whenever we create together, the true magic happens. It's a gift to learn from her and all the many hats she's worn: sister, daughter, mother, friend, teacher, dean, project manager, innovator, Captain of Fun, and so much more. And let me just say, if it's not clear, I'm extremely proud of my sister, Dr. Alishea Jurado." –Frank (Mr. J), co-author and brother

ELLIE BEYKZADEH

Ellie is an Iranian-American illustrator with published works based in the vibrant city of Chicago. Her belief in finding beauty across the globe fuels her creative spirit. Armed with a BFA in visual arts – painting, and backed by dual MA's in Art Research and Arts Management, she's delved into various mediums and styles, channeling a distinct vision into each project. Her illustrations weave a whimsical tapestry, entwining her journeys, personal moments, and the enchanting essence of everyday life. Guided by a passion for capturing the magic and curiosity of childhood, she infuses her art with the spirit of adventure, inviting young readers to embark on imaginative explorations of their own. Join her on Instagram @elliecolorss, or visit elliecolors.com to embark on this artistic journey together.

Milton Keynes UK
Ingram Content Group UK Ltd.
UKHW050612091123
432236UK00003B/67